Black Beauty

*Retold from the Anna Sewell
original by Lisa Church*

Illustrated by Lucy Corvino

Sterling Publishing Co., Inc.
New York

2   4   6   8   10   9   7   5   3   1

Published by Sterling Publishing Co., Inc.
387 Park Avenue South, New York, NY 10016
Copyright © 2005 by Lisa Church
Illustrations copyright © 2005 by Lucy Corvino
Distributed in Canada by Sterling Publishing
$^c/_o$ Canadian Manda Group, 165 Dufferin Street
Toronto, Ontario, Canada M6K 3H6
Distributed in Great Britain and Europe by Chris Lloyd at Orca Book
Services, Stanley House, Fleets Lane, Poole BH15 3AJ, England
Distributed in Australia by Capricorn Link (Australia) Pty. Ltd.
P.O. Box 704, Windsor, NSW 2756, Australia

Printed in China
All Rights Reserved
Design by Renato Stanisic

Sterling ISBN 1-4027-2264-8

CONTENTS

PART I

CHAPTER 1

My Early Years

The first place I remember was a large, pleasant meadow. On this land, there was a clear pond. Shady trees leaned over the water. A plowed field was to our left and our master's house was to our right. It was a beautiful place.

When I was very young, I stayed by my mother. As I grew older, she would work during the day and come back in the evening.

I ran and played with six colts in the meadow, but sometimes the other colts would kick and bite.

"Listen to what I say," my mother said one day. "These colts are cart-horse colts. They have not learned manners. You have been well bred. Your parents and grandparents have good tempers. You have never seen me kick or bite. I hope you will grow up gentle and good. Never learn bad ways. Do your work without complaining. Lift your feet high when you trot. And never bite or kick, even when it's only play."

I have never forgotten my mother's words. She was a wise mare, and our master liked her very much. He called her Pet, even though her name was Duchess.

When our master came to the gate, my mother neighed with joy and ran to him. As I was dull black, he called me Darkie. He would give me bread and my mother would get a carrot.

Before I was two years old, something happened that I have never forgotten.

We were eating in the meadow when the

2

oldest of the colts said, "There are the hounds!"

"They have found a rabbit," said my mother, who was standing nearby. Soon men on horseback galloped by as fast as they could. They were far into the lower field when the dogs stopped running and barking.

"They must have lost the scent," said another old horse, watching the dogs scatter with their noses to the ground. "Perhaps the rabbit will get away."

Before long, the dogs started yowling and came back toward us at full speed. A rabbit rushed by, wild with fright. The dogs burst over the bank, leaped the stream, and came dashing across the field. The men followed.

The rabbit tried to get through a fence but couldn't. She turned toward the road, but the yowling dogs were too quick. Then, we heard a shriek and that was the end of her.

I was so surprised that I didn't see what was

going on by the brook. Two fine horses were down, one in the stream, the other one in the grass. One rider got out of the stream; the other man lay still.

Later we learned that George Gordon, the Squire's only son, had died in the accident.

As we watched, one of the horses lay on the grass, badly injured. One man left and came back with a gun, and after a loud bang, all was still.

The black horse moved no more. My mother seemed upset and sad. She said she knew that horse for a long time, and that Rob Roy was a good horse. After that day, my mother never visited that part of the field again.

My master took care of me until I turned four. That was when Squire Gordon came to look at me. He looked at my eyes, my mouth, and my legs and then watched me walk, trot, and gallop. My coat was soft and bright black. I had one white foot and a pretty white star on my forehead.

"When he is broken in, he will do very well," the man said. Broken in meant that I would wear a saddle and bridle and carry a man, woman, or child on my back. It meant I would listen to my master's commands. I also had to understand that when my harness was on, I could neither jump for joy nor lie down.

I had much to learn. The worst thing was getting used to the bit and bridle. But with kind words from my master and a bucket of oats, I allowed it to be worn. My master took me to a blacksmith, who fitted me for shoes made of iron. They didn't hurt, but my feet felt very stiff and heavy.

I also learned to wear a collar on my neck and blinkers around my eyes that allowed me to only look straight ahead. Even my tail was bothered. A small saddle with a strap forced my tail to double up and poke out of a small hole. I never felt more like kicking! But of course, I did not kick

5

my kind master. In time, I got used to everything.

Then my master sent me to a neighbor's farm for two weeks. I was in a meadow with sheep and cows, feeding quietly. A long black train came, puffing out billows of smoke. I was scared at first, but during the day, many other trains went by. The cows kept eating quietly, hardly raising their heads. And so I began to ignore the trains just as the cows and sheep did.

After learning how to drive a carriage, I was finally broken in. I was ready to go to my new master. My mother told me there are many kinds of men: some are good, but many are foolish. She hoped that I would fall into good hands. However, a horse never knows who may buy him or who may drive him. It is all a matter of chance. "But still," said Mother, "you must do your best wherever you are, and keep up your good name."

CHAPTER 2

A Fair Start

⌒

In early May, a man took me to my new home at Squire Gordon's. The barn I was taken to was very roomy. I was placed in the first box since the other three stalls were smaller. It was called a loose box, because the horse that was put into it was not tied up. The man gave me some nice oats, patted me, spoke kindly, and went away.

I looked in the stall next to mine, where a little fat gray pony stood, and said, "How do you do? What is your name?"

He turned around as far as his rope would

allow and said, "My name is Merrylegs. Are you going to live next door to me?"

"Yes," I said.

"Well, then," he said. "I hope you have a good temper. I do not like anyone next door who bites."

Just then a tall chestnut mare, a beautiful brown horse, spoke to me. "So you're the colt that's made me leave my home!"

"I'm sorry," I said, "but I had nothing to do with that. A man brought me here. I've never had a fight before, and I don't want to start one now."

"Well," she said, "we shall see."

I said nothing back to her.

In the afternoon, the mare went out and Merrylegs told me all about her.

"Ginger has a bad habit of biting. One day, she bit James in the arm! Miss Flora and Miss Jessie, the ones who ride me and love me so much, used to bring me apples and carrots. Now I hope they will come again, if you don't bite."

I told Merrylegs I never bit and I couldn't think of why Ginger would do such a thing.

"Well, she says she bites because no one was ever kind to her. But the men here treat her well. She might be fine now."

Merrylegs continued. "I am twelve years old, and I can tell you that there is not a better place for a horse than right here. John has been here fourteen years and is the best trainer around. And you'll never see a kinder boy than James. So don't worry. It is all Ginger's fault that she did not stay in that box."

In the cottage near the stables lived John Manly, our coachman. My first morning there, the Squire saw me and told John to take me for a run. At first John rode me slowly, then at a trot, and then at a fine gallop. When we met up with the Squire and his wife, our master asked, "Well John, how does he go?"

"He is as quick as a deer! With the lightest touch of the reins, he goes. We went near where they were shooting rabbits. At the sound of guns, he was steady. It's my guess that he was not frightened or hit when he was young."

The next day, the Squire took me for a run. When we returned, he said he never met a more pleasant animal. "What shall we call him?" he asked his wife.

"I don't know," she said. "He is really quite a beauty, and he has such a sweet face and fine, intelligent eyes. How do you like the name Black Beauty?"

"I think that's a wonderful name!" the Squire said.

John took me back to the stable, telling James of my new name.

"If I had my choice," James said, "I would have called him Rob Roy. I have never seen two horses so much alike."

"That's no wonder," John said. "Didn't you know that Farmer Grey's old Duchess was the mother of both of them?"

I had never heard that before. I now knew that Rob Roy, the horse that was killed at that hunt, was my brother! No wonder my mother was so upset.

A few days after this, I went out with Ginger in the carriage. I was happy to learn that she worked hard at her job. She did her fair share, making our trips very enjoyable.

Merrylegs and I soon became great friends. He was such a cheerful, good-tempered pony! Miss Jessie and Miss Flora would ride him in the orchard and play games.

Our master had two other horses.

Justice was used mainly for riding. The other horse was named Sir Oliver and he was the master's favorite. We chatted occasionally, but I never got to know these horses as well as I did Ginger.

CHAPTER 3

Ginger and Merrylegs

෴

Now I had to stand up in a stable night and day, except when someone wanted me to work. There were days when I was so full of life that I really could not keep quiet. I jumped and danced and pranced around.

There were a few times we had our freedom. The carriage never went out on Sundays, so we were turned out into the fields or the orchard. We galloped, rolled over on our backs, and nibbled on the sweet grass. We were talking together under the shade of the large chestnut tree when Ginger began her story.

"I was taken from my mother early and put with other colts. The man who took care of us never gave me a kind word. I was a high-spirited horse, and needed time to exercise. Instead, I was shut up in a stall, day after day. I cried to get loose, but no one would listen. There was one old master, who seemed rather nice, but he had turned the work over to his son, Samson.

"One morning, he tried to put a new bit in my mouth. It hurt so much! I must have made Samson angry, because he hit me hard with the rein. I reared up on my two hind legs, making him even madder. He began to beat me, so I tried kicking him. Then, I galloped off to the end of the field where I stood under an oak tree and waited, but no one came to get me. The sun grew hot and I felt hungry, but there was not enough grass in that meadow. I longed to lie down, but the saddle was still strapped on. I wanted a drink, but there wasn't a drop in sight.

"As the sun went down, the old master came out. He spoke gently to me: 'Come along, girl, come along.' He stayed by my side and petted me while I ate the oats. He saw the blood on my side where his son had hit me. Then he led me quietly to the stable where Samson was waiting.

"'You have hurt this horse!' he warned his son. 'From now on, stay away from her!'

"The old master then took off my saddle and bridle and sponged me down with care. My back hurt. My mouth felt so bad that I couldn't eat the hay. But my master's words were sweet and soothing. After that, he often came to see me. He also gave another man the job of training me. I soon learned what he wanted from me."

Then Ginger told me more about the first place she lived. "After my breaking in, I was bought by a dealer to match another brown horse. Then we were sold to a rich gentleman in London. Since we were taken to fashionable places in town, we had to wear a bearing rein. It made us hold our heads up higher to look down on others.

"When we went to a grand party, we waited for hours. If I stamped my foot, I was hit with a whip. You see, our master only wanted us to look good. The driver of the carriage said I was a mean-tempered horse and soon I became one. I always had pain in my neck and I began to kick when anyone came to harness me. Finally, they sent me somewhere else."

I felt bad for Ginger, but as time went on, she became more gentle and cheerful. One day James even said, "I do think that mare is starting to like me."

John answered. "Soon she will be as pleasant as Black Beauty. All it takes is kindness."

Mr. Blomefield, a friend of our master, had a large family. Sometimes his children would come and play with Miss Jessie and Miss Flora. When they came, everyone wanted to ride Merrylegs.

One afternoon, he had been out with them a long time. James brought him back to the stable, scolding him all the way.

"What have you been doing, Merrylegs?" I asked.

"Oh!" he said, "I taught those children a lesson! They didn't understand that I was getting tired, so I just pitched them off backward. That was the only way they were going to understand."

"What?" I said. "Did you throw Miss Jessie or Miss Flora?"

"Of course not!" he said. "I am very careful with the young ladies and the little children. It is the boys who are upsetting! Even though I was tired, I galloped them about the orchard, putting up with their whips made of sticks. When I could go no more, I stopped. When they took me back to James, they were still carrying their big sticks. He knew what had happened, and he blamed them instead of me."

"If I had been you," said Ginger, "I would have given those boys a good kick!"

"I'm sure you would have," said Merrylegs, "but I would not like to make my master or James ashamed of me. They trust me with the children as much as they trust themselves. I love them too much to hurt them. Besides, if I kicked one of those children, I would be sold in a jiffy, probably to someone not nearly as nice. I hope I shall never have to leave here!"

CHAPTER 4

Horse Sense

Our greatest pleasure was when we were saddled for a riding party. The master got on Ginger, the mistress on me, and the young ladies on Sir Oliver and Merrylegs. We cheerfully trotted about together. The mistress was light, her voice sweet, and her hand so light on the reins that I was guided almost without feeling it.

One day, after one of our rides together, I asked Sir Oliver why his tail was so short. It was only six or seven inches long. I inquired what accident could have caused it.

"Accident?" he snorted with a fierce look. "It was no accident! It was cold-blooded cruelty. When I was young, I was taken to a place where they cut off my tail, clear through to the bone!"

"How dreadful!" I exclaimed.

"Dreadful, yes, it was dreadful! The pain was terrible and lasted a long time. What a torment it is when the flies settle on you and sting and sting and you have no way to brush them off. Thank goodness they don't cut off tails anymore."

"Why did they do it then?" asked Ginger.

"For looks, for fashion," said the old horse, stamping his foot. "There weren't any well-bred horses in my time that didn't have their tails shortened."

"I suppose it is fashion that makes them in London strap our heads up with those horrid metal bits," said Ginger.

"Of course it is," he said. "It is not right!"

Merrylegs agreed with our comments, and then had a question of his own.

"Can anyone tell me what blinkers are for?" Merrylegs had never understood why horses were fitted with black eye patches.

"They are supposed to keep horses from getting scared," answered Justice, a friendly horse in the field. "They are meant to keep horses looking toward the front so they don't cause an accident."

"I think," said Sir Oliver, "that blinkers are dangerous in the night. We horses can see much better in the dark than man can."

"Can't they see the way God has made us and meant for us to be?" Ginger asked.

Merrylegs thought that was enough talk for the day. So he led us to the orchard, where we munched on the apples that lay on the grass.

One day in late autumn, I was pulling the dog-cart. This was an easy cart to pull: it was light, and the high wheels ran along so smoothly. There had been a lot of rain, and we went merrily along until we came to the low wooden bridge.

The man at the gate before the bridge said the river was rising fast. Many of the meadows were underwater. In one low part of the road, the water was halfway up to my knees! However, my master drove me gently and we made it.

When we got to the town, my master's business lasted a long time. By this time, the rain was coming down hard. I heard my master tell John this was the worst storm he had ever been in. The branches were swaying and the roaring sound was terrible.

"I wish we were out of these woods," said my master. Then we heard a groan, a crack, and a splitting sound. An oak tree crashed down in the road before us. I stopped still and trembled.

"What shall we do now?" my master asked.

"We must go back to the other road and try the wooden bridge," John answered.

So back we went. But the moment my feet touched the first part of the bridge, I knew there

was something wrong. I came to a dead stop and would not move.

"Go on, Beauty," said my master.

"There's something wrong, sir," said John.

"Come on, Beauty, what's the matter?" Of course I couldn't tell him, but I knew that the bridge was not safe.

Just then, the man from the gate ran out of the house, swinging a lit torch for us to see. "Hello! Stop!" he cried. "The bridge is broken in the middle! If you try to move forward, you'll be swept away and drowned!"

"Thank goodness!" said my master.

"You Beauty!" said John. He took my bridle that I wore on my nose and gently turned me around. The wind seemed to have calmed some, though it was still dark. I trotted quietly along.

I could hear my master and John talking quietly. I heard John say that if we had moved forward, the river would have washed us all away. He said that God had given men reason to find out things, but he had given animals the sense to know about things more quickly and surely than men. He had many stories to tell about animals that had saved men's lives.

At last we came to the gates of our home. The gardener was standing at the entrance, looking out for us. The mistress had been frantic with worry that we had been in an accident. She had sent James off on Justice to find us.

We saw a light at the hall door and at the upper windows. "Are you really safe, my dear?" my mistress called out as we approached.

"Yes, my dear. But if your Black Beauty had not been wiser than we were, we should all have been carried away in the river."

I heard no more because they walked into the house and John took me to the stable. Oh, what a good supper I had that night: bran mash and crushed beans with my oats! And John softened my stable with thick straw. I was very glad, for I was tired from our long day.

CHAPTER 5

A Little Devil

One day, John and I were out on some business of our master's. We saw a boy trying to make his pony leap over a gate. The pony would not jump over the high gate, though the boy hit him hard with a whip. The boy, angry because his pony wouldn't listen, got down off the pony and hit him several times in the head. He got up on the animal again, and whipped him hard and kicked him. Still the pony wouldn't jump.

When we got very near the two, we saw the pony put his head down and throw up his heels.

He kicked so hard he sent the boy over a hedge.

"Serves you right!" John laughed out loud.

"Come help me!" called the boy.

"Maybe being thrown into the hedges will teach you a lesson. You shouldn't jump a pony over a gate that is too high for him."

The boy seemed all right, and John and I rode off. On the way, though, John decided to stop off at Farmer Bushby's to tell him about the boy's cruelty to the pony. When we arrived, the farmer and his wife were hurrying onto the road, looking very frightened.

"Have you seen my boy?" asked Mr. Bushby. "He went out an hour ago on my black pony, and the animal has just come back without him!"

"The poor pony is better off without a rider," John replied. "Your son should not be riding a pony if he can't treat it fairly."

"What do you mean?" asked the farmer.

"Well, I saw your son whipping and kicking

and punching that little pony simply because he wouldn't leap a gate that was too high for him. The pony behaved well and tried its best, but finally he could take it no more. He kicked up his heels and threw the boy off. Your son wanted me to help him, but I'm sorry to say, I didn't feel like helping. Don't worry—he didn't break any bones. He only has a few scratches. But I love horses, and it upsets me to see them badly used."

The mother began to cry. "Oh, my poor Bill! I must go and meet him. He must be hurt."

"Go inside, dear," the man said to his wife. "Bill needs to be taught a lesson. This is not the first time he has been mean to that animal."

Then to John, he said, "Thank you so for telling me, sir." Later I heard John say something about cruelty being the devil's trademark.

John and I went home, happy to have helped that poor pony.

One morning early in December, my master came into the stable carrying a letter in his hand. "Come here, James," said the master. "I have a letter from my brother-in-law, Sir Clifford Williams of Clifford Hall. His coachman, who has cared for his horses for years, is getting old. He wants a younger man to learn the job. He would pay you well and it would be a good start, although I would hate to lose you."

John looked his way. "I would hate to lose you, as well, James. But I would never stand in your way for the world."

A few days after this conversation, it was settled that James should go to Clifford Hall in a month. Everyone was sure he would be wonderful at his new job.

CHAPTER 6

The Fire

Before James was to leave, my master and mistress decided to visit some friends who lived some distance away. James was to drive them. As the sun went down, we stopped at a hotel and dropped off my master and mistress. James drove us to the stable, and two men came out to take care of us. The little man in charge was a pleasant person. I never saw anyone unbuckle a harness as quickly as he did. With a pat and a kind word, he led me to a long stable housing two or three horses. The other man brought Ginger.

I never was cleaned so quickly as by that little old man. When he was done, James petted me, thinking the man might not have done a very good job. But he found my coat as clean and smooth as silk.

"Practice makes perfect," said the little old man. "After forty years of practice, I should be doing everything right!" James laughed with him. They conversed about how to train horses. James was pleased to hear that the old man thought as he did.

"Train them as you would children," James said. "That's what we believe."

"Who is your master, young man?"

"Squire Gordon, of Birtwick Park," James answered.

"Ah, I have heard of him. He is a fine judge of horses. Some say he is the best rider in the country!"

"I believe he is," replied James. "But he rides

very little now, since his son was killed."

"I read all about it in the newspaper," the man remarked. "Wasn't there a fine horse killed, too?"

"Yes," said James, "a splendid creature! He was a brother of this fine horse here."

James pointed to me.

"That's a shame!" said the old man. "It was a bad place to leap, if I remember correctly. I like to go on a hunt as much as any other man, but no foxtail is worth the life of a young man and a fine horse."

James nodded his head sadly in agreement. When they finished grooming us, they left the stable together, still talking about Rob Roy.

Later on that evening, another traveler's horse was put in the stall next to mine. While the groomer was brushing the horse, a young man smoking a pipe walked in. I could tell they were friends.

"Hey, Towler," said the groomer, "run up the

ladder into the loft and throw some hay down into this horse's stall. But lay down your pipe before you go up there."

"All right," said the young man. By the time he got finished, James had come to say good night. The doors were locked, and the two men left.

I can't say how long I slept, but I woke up suddenly and put my nose up to smell. The air seemed thick. Ginger was coughing, and one of the other horses was moving about restlessly. I heard a rushing noise, and a low crackling and snapping sound. I didn't know what it was, but it made me tremble all over. The other horses were all awake now. They pulled at their halters and were stamping their feet.

At last I heard steps outside. The groomer burst into the stable with a lantern and began to untie the horses, trying to lead them out. The first horse would not go out with him. Finally he left the stable alone. I guess we were all foolish, but there was nobody we knew we could trust.

Then I heard a cry of "Fire!" outside. The little old man who had groomed me so well showed up quickly. He came in the barn and led one horse out, but the flames were now roaring overhead dreadfully.

The next thing I heard was James' voice, quiet and cheery as he always was.

"Come, my beauties, it is time for us to be off, so wake up and come along." I stood nearest the door, so he came to me first, patting me as he came in.

Quickly, he took the scarf off his neck and tied it lightly over my eyes. Then, he led me out of the stable. I whinnied as loud as I could, trying to get Ginger to come out.

James continued bringing the horses out one by one. There was shouting, and I could see black smoke pouring out thicker than ever. In the middle of this mess, I heard my master's voice call out, "James! James! Are you there?"

There was no answer, but I heard a crash of something falling in the stable. The next moment I gave a loud, joyful neigh. I saw James coming through the smoke, leading Ginger out with him. She told me later that my whinnying was the best thing I could have done. If she had not heard me outside, she never would have come out.

A sound of galloping horses and rumbling wheels caused everyone to look around. "It's the fire engine!" shouted two or three people. The firemen leaped to the ground just as we got away from the building.

Later we found out that the young man who had been in the barn earlier had left his pipe there, and the hay had caught fire. Ginger and I were so lucky to have been saved from that fire. We would always be grateful to James for saving our lives.

CHAPTER 7

Going for the Doctor

∽

The rest of our journey was easy. By sunset, we had reached the house of my master's friend. We were taken into a clean, snug stable. A kind coachman there made us very comfortable. He had already heard about James' bravery.

"One thing is very clear, young man," he said. "Your horses know who they can trust. It is one of the hardest things in the world to get horses out of a stable when there is either a fire or flood. I don't know why they won't come out, but they won't."

We stayed three days at this place and then headed for home. We were glad to be in our own stable again, and John was glad to see us as well. Later, I heard John talking to James about who would replace him.

"Little Joe Green?" James said. "He's a child and such a little fellow!"

"He is fourteen and a half," said John. "Yes, he is small, but he is kind, too. And his father thinks it is a wonderful chance for him." John made it sound like a great idea.

"You are a good man!" said James. "I only hope I can be like you someday."

"My life has not always been this good, James. When I was just as old as Joe Green, my parents died of the fever. The master took me into the stable, and Norman the coachman was told to teach me. Norman could have told the master that I was too young to help. Instead, he was like a father to me. When Norman died a few years after that, I took his place. So you see, James, little Joe and I will do just fine. There's nothing like showing kindness to someone who needs it."

"You have been my best friend," said James. "I hope you won't forget me."

The next day Joe came to the stable to learn all he could before James left. He learned to sweep the stable, bring in straw and hay, clean a harness, and wash the carriages.

At last the day came when James had to leave us. He was not his usual cheerful self, but John gave him a smile. "You will make new friends, James. And you will be good at your job." John's words cheered James up.

He left us with a wave and a slight smile. Merrylegs cried for several days. Each morning as Ginger and I trotted and galloped, John talked Merrylegs into better spirits. In the end, we felt better about James leaving. We would grow to love Joe just as well.

One night, soon after James had left, John suddenly unlocked the stable doors and came in calling, "Wake up, Beauty! You must take off now to Doctor White's!"

John took me quickly up to the main house, where the Squire stood with a lamp in his hand. "John, ride as fast as you can for your mistress' sake!" my master said. "Give Beauty a rest at the inn and come back as soon as you can."

I galloped as fast as I could. The air was frosty and the moon was bright. After ten miles of running, we came to Doctor White's door. John rang the bell twice and then a window was opened. Doctor White put his head out and said, "What do you want?"

"Mrs. Gordon is very sick, sir. The master wants you to go at once."

"Wait," he said, "but I will have to borrow your horse."

"All right," John said as he stood by me and

stroked my neck. I was very hot. The doctor soon came back out and we left, leaving John far behind.

The doctor was not a very good rider. He stopped once to let me catch my breath. Shortly after our break, we made it to the main house.

My master had heard us coming. He didn't say a word, but only opened the door and let the doctor in. Joe led me to the stable. My legs were shaking under me and I could only stand and pant.

Poor Joe tried his best. He rubbed my legs and my chest, but he didn't put my warm blanket on me. He thought I was too hot. Then he gave me a full pail of water to drink. It was cold and delicious, and I drank it all. Then he gave me hay and corn and, thinking he had done a good job, he went away. I grew very cold and I ached all over. Oh, how I wished for my warm, thick blanket as I stood and trembled. I wished for John, but he had ten miles to walk, so I tried to sleep.

After a long while, I heard John at the door. I gave a low moan, for I was in great pain. He covered me up with two or three warm blankets, and then ran to the house for some hot water. He made me some warm grain mixture, which I ate, and then I went to sleep.

John seemed to be very angry. I heard him say to himself, "Stupid boy! No blanket put on!" and "Water too cold!" Even so, I knew Joe had done his best.

I was very sick now. An infection had attacked my lungs, and I couldn't take a breath without pain. I do not know how long I was ill. Mr. Bond, the horse doctor, came every day. One day he bled me; John held a pail for the blood. I felt very faint after it and thought I would die, and I believe they all thought so, too.

Ginger and Merrylegs had been moved into the other stable so that I might have some quiet. The fever had made me very quick of hearing. Any little noise seemed quite loud, and I could detect everyone's footsteps going to and from the house. I knew everything that was going on.

John would get up two or three times a night to come to me. My master visited, too. "My poor Beauty," he said. "You are such a good horse. You saved your mistress' life."

I was very glad to hear that. It seemed the doctor had said that if my mistress had gone longer without medicine, she would have died.

One night, Tom Green, Joe's father, came to help John give me my medicine. Then they sat down nearby to talk.

"I wish you would say a kind word to Joe," the older man said. "He says he knows it was his fault, though he did the best he could."

After a short time, John said slowly, "Tom, I

know he didn't mean to do any harm. But you see, that horse is the pride of my heart. I will try to give him a kind word tomorrow—but only if Beauty is better."

"Thank you, John. I know you don't mean to be hard on the boy. You're just not thinking clearly—you are ignorant."

John's answer startled me. "How can you say that? If people can say, 'Oh, I didn't know, I didn't mean any harm,' they think it's all right. Remember when those young ladies left the door open on your garden house and your plants were killed by the cold? And yet, the young ladies didn't mean it. It was only ignorance!"

I didn't hear any more of this conversation, for the medicine started to work and I got very sleepy. In the morning I felt much better, but I often thought of John's words that night.

CHAPTER 8

The Parting

Joe Green did very well. He learned quickly and was so careful that John began to trust him with many things.

One morning, the master wanted a note taken right away to a gentleman's house. The note was being delivered when we saw a cart loaded down with bricks. The wheels were stuck in the mud, and the man who was with it was shouting and whipping the two horses quite hard.

"Hey!" said Joe as he pulled up near them.

"Don't go hitting those horses like that!" The man paid no attention.

"Stop, please, stop!" Joe yelled again. "I'll help you lighten the cart."

"Mind your own business, little boy!" the man said as he started to hit the horses even harder.

The next moment, we were off to the main house to get the master brickmaker. The house was by the road, and Mr. Clay himself came out.

"Hello, young man. You seem in a hurry. Has the Squire sent you?"

"No, Mr. Clay, but there's a fellow in your brickyard whipping two horses to death. I told him to stop, but he wouldn't. Please go." Joe's voice shook with anger.

"Thank you, young man," the man said as he went off to find the fellow and Joe headed for home. When Joe arrived, he told John how the man was treating the horses.

"You did the right thing, Joe," John said, patting him on the back. "Many folks would have ridden by and minded their own business."

Rubbing me down and cleaning my shoes helped to calm Joe down. He was just going home when a man came down to the stable to say that Joe was wanted right away in the master's private room.

We heard afterward that the man who had whipped the horses so badly could possibly spend two or three months in jail.

There was a great change in Joe after that day. John said he jumped at once from being a boy to becoming a man. I always felt safe with Joe after that day. I knew that he'd always protect me from harm.

From time to time our mistress was ill and the doctor was often at the house. Then we heard that she must leave her home to move to a warmer climate. We all felt sad as the master began immediately making plans to leave England.

John went about his work silently and sadly, and Joe hardly ever whistled anymore.

The first ones in the family to leave were Miss Jessie and Miss Flora. They came to bid us goodbye and hugged poor Merrylegs like an old friend. Then we heard that our master had sold Ginger and me to an old friend. He thought we would be happy there. Merrylegs was given to the Blomefields. But it was to be understood that he should never be sold, but used only for the enjoyment of the children.

Joe followed Merrylegs to the Blomefields to take care of him and help in the house. I thought Merrylegs would do fine. John had several choices of where he could go. He was going to look around a bit before making a choice.

The evening before he left, the master came

into the stable to give some directions and give his horses one last pat.

"Have you decided what to do, John?" he said. "I know you have many offers."

"No, sir," he said. "I know I want to train horses, though."

"I don't know any man more suited for training them," said the master. "If I can help you in any way, write to me."

Master gave John his new address and then thanked him for his years of work. They parted sadly, hoping to see one another again someday.

Soon, the last sad day came for me as well. I watched as the master carried his wife out to the carriage. When we reached the railway station, the master and our mistress gave us all teary good-byes. Even Joe stood close to us to hide his tears. Then, the doors of the train slammed shut and the whistle blew. The train glided away, leaving behind only clouds of white smoke and some very heavy hearts.

When it was out of sight, John came back.

"We shall never see her again," he said as he took the reins alongside Joe and drove slowly home. But it wasn't our home anymore.

PART II

CHAPTER 9

Learning New Ways

❧

The next morning, Joe said good-bye to us, and Merrylegs neighed to us from the yard. Then John put the saddle on Ginger and the leading rein on me, and rode us about fifteen miles to Earlshall Park. We went into the yard through a stone gateway, and John asked for Mr. York.

Mr. York was a fine-looking middle-aged man, and his voice was the type horses knew they must obey. He was very friendly, though, and polite to John. After looking over Ginger and me, he called a groomer to take us to our stable. He then invited John in for a cool drink.

We were taken to a light, airy stable and placed in adjoining stalls. We were rubbed down and then fed. In about half an hour, John and Mr. York, who was to be our new coachman, came in to see us.

The man spoke to John firmly: "I can see nothing wrong simply by looking at these horses, but we both know that horses are all very singular and need different treatments. Is there anything about these two you think you ought to tell me?"

"Well," said John, "I don't believe there is a better pair of horses in the whole country. The black one has never heard a harsh word or been hit in his life. He will do just about anything you ask. But the brown chestnut does get in a bad mood now and then. If she were mistreated, she would probably act mean in return."

"I will remember what you have said," the coachman replied.

"Oh, there is one other thing," John said before walking away. "We have never used the bearing rein with either of them. The black horse never had one on, and it was the gag-bit that gave the chestnut such a bad temper."

"Well," said Mr. York, "they will have to wear the bearing rein. The mistress loves style. But I will only use it when my lady rides."

As John patted us for the last time, his voice was very sad.

I held my face close to him. That was all I could do to say good-bye. And then he was gone, and I have never seen him since.

The next day, my new master, whom everyone called "Lord," came over to look at us.

"I have a good feeling about these horses," he said. "My old friend, Mr. Gordon, treated them well. Of course their colors don't match, but as long as we are in the country, that will do."

Mr. York told him what John had said about us.

"Well," he said, "you keep an eye on the mare. We'll start her out easy on the bearing rein."

In the afternoon, we were harnessed and hooked to the carriage. Two footmen were standing ready in front of the house, dressed in very plain clothes. Then I heard the sound of silk rustling as my lady came down the stone steps. A tall woman got in the carriage without saying a word.

This was the first time I had ever worn a bearing rein. I wasn't able to put my head down, but the rein didn't pull it up any higher than I was used to carrying it.

The next day at three o'clock, we were again at the door, waiting for our lady. We soon heard the silk dress and her mean voice. "Mr. York! You must put those horses' heads higher! They look awful."

Mr. York got down and said shyly, "I am sorry, my lady, but my Lord said to raise their heads a little at a time. But if you say so, I can take them up a little more."

"I do say so!" she said.

Mr. York came around to our heads and shortened the rein himself. My head went up higher, bothering me as soon as he did it. I was able to stand it, until we came to a steep hill. I had to pull the carriage with my head up now, and it hurt my back and legs.

Ginger said, "We are treated well here. However, if they make my head go up any higher, I will fight it!"

Day by day, our bearing reins were tightened, making our heads go up a little bit on each ride. I now dreaded putting my harness on. Every day, I thought the worst had to be over. Little did I know, the worst was yet to come. One day, my lady came down later than usual.

"Drive me to my friend's, the Duchess," she said. "And get those horses' heads up! Raise them the whole way now!"

Mr. York drew my head back and fixed the rein so tightly I could hardly stand it. Then he went to Ginger. She was already raising her head up and down, fighting the man before he even started. When Mr. York took off the rein to shorten it, Ginger reared up on her hind legs. Mr. York and the groomer flew to her head, but she went on rearing and kicking. At last she knocked over the carriage and fell down, kicking me harshly as she went down. Mr. York sat on her head and yelled directions, trying to make the whole mess go away.

The groomer led me to my box. Then he ran to help Mr. York. I stood still, but my mood was miserable. Before long, Ginger was brought into the stable by two groomers. She looked like she had been hit quite hard.

The men were upset by what had happened. They said, "If our lady hadn't insisted on those bearing reins being so tight, this never would have happened! I'm sure our Lord is going to be angry. But if he can't make his wife see what's right, we surely can't!"

Mr. York felt me all over, looking for the place where I had been kicked. He soon found it. He ordered it to be sponged with hot water and then had lotion put on.

Our Lord was upset and blamed Mr. York for listening to his mistress. He said that from now on, all orders came only from him.

Ginger was never put in the carriage again, but when her bruises healed, she was given to one of the Lord's youngest sons. He was sure she would make a good hunter. As for me, I still had to pull the carriage. I was teamed with another horse, named Max. He was used to a tight rein because he had worn one since he was young. I asked him how he stood it.

"Well," he said, "I wear one only because I have to. They are very bad for us."

"Do you think our masters know that?" I asked.

"I don't know. But the doctors do. I heard them talking once. They said the London people always want the heads of their horses held high. It is bad for the horses but good for fashion."

I can't even begin to describe how much it hurt to be in that bearing rein for those four long months. The sharp bit on my tongue made my mouth foam. The high tilt of my head made it hard for me to breathe, too. After a carriage ride, my neck and chest were strained and painful. I felt worn out and sad.

In my old home, I always knew that John and my master were my friends. How I wished for a friend to look out for me!

CHAPTER 10

Reuben Smith

⚬

Reuben Smith was left in charge of the stables when Mr. York went to London. He was a very smart man and was gentle with us. Most men with his smart ways would have been coachmen like Mr. York.

It was now early in April and the family was to be coming home sometime in May. Mr. Smith was to drive the carriage into town and get it all fixed up. He was to take me with him so he could ride me home after he dropped it off.

We left the carriage at the maker's, and Smith

rode me to the White Lion Inn, where I could rest and eat. There, the man was told to feed me well and ready me for the trip home at four o'clock.

After I ate, I was being rubbed down when the man found a nail loose in one of my front shoes. Later that afternoon, when Reuben Smith found out about the nail, he told the man I would be fine till he got home. He left again, saying he had met some friends and he would be back soon.

He spoke in a loud voice, which was quite unlike him. Letting the nail go until we got home was not something he would usually do, either. His decision surprised me. It was nearly nine o'clock when he finally came. He seemed in a very bad mood, and he yelled loudly at the man who was keeping me.

The man who owned the stables stood at the door, and Reuben Smith yelled at him, too. He got on my back and put me into a full gallop even before we got out of town. It was very dark and the roads were stony, making my loose shoe become even looser. Finally it came off.

Reuben Smith paid no attention to the road or to me. A long road up ahead was covered with large, sharp stones that no horse should be driven over quickly. With no shoe on, the road would be very dangerous for me. When Reuben Smith made me gallop, I was frightened. But he kept hitting me with the whip, and wanted me to go even faster! Of course, my shoeless foot hurt terribly. The hoof was broken and split, the inside cut painfully by the sharp stones.

No horse could keep his footing on this road. The pain was too great. I stumbled and fell down hard on my knees. I flung Smith off my back as I fell. At the speed we were going, he must have fallen quite hard himself. I soon got back on my feet and limped to the side of the road where there were no stones. I could see Reuben Smith lying a few yards beyond me, but he didn't get up.

He tried once, but gave a great groan and fell back on the road.

I could have groaned, too, for I was in great pain from both my foot and knees. But horses are used to living through their pain in silence. I made no sound, but just stood there and listened. The only sounds were a few low notes of a nightingale. Nothing moved but the white clouds near the moon, and the brown owl that flitted over the hedges.

It was sometime in the middle of the night when I heard the sound of horse's feet. As the sound came nearer, I neighed loudly and was thrilled to hear an answering neigh from Ginger and the din of men's voices. They came slowly over the stones and stopped to see the man lying on the ground.

"It's Reuben!" said one of the men as he bent over him. "He's dead!"

"His horse must have thrown him. Who

would have thought that this black horse would do such a thing?" the other man asked.

The same man tried to lead me forward. I took a step, but almost fell again.

"Whoa!" the man said in a surprised voice. "Look at this horse! His knees are bleeding and his hoof is cut to pieces, poor fellow! Reuben should have known not to ride him over these stones without a shoe. He must have been drinking in town; otherwise, he would not have done it!"

"His poor wife!" one of the men said. "She sent me to come and find him."

I will never forget that night walk. It was more than three miles long. One man took off slowly with the body in the cart. The other man led me as I limped along in great pain. He kept patting me and said such nice words to me.

At last I reached my stable, where I got some corn. The man wrapped up my knees in wet bandages. He then tied my foot in a wrap filled with medicine to take the pain away. The next day, the doctor said he hoped my joint was not hurt.

I went through a lot of pain in the days to come. Reuben's wife did, too. If only Reuben Smith could have stayed away from that cursed drink. We all would have been better off.

CHAPTER 11

Job Horses

◌∽

As soon as my knees were healed, I was turned out to a beautiful small meadow for a month or two. I missed Ginger and neighed when I heard horses in the distance, but I rarely got an answer back.

One morning, the gate was opened, and who should come in but Ginger. With a joyful whinny, I trotted up to her. But Ginger was not there to keep me company. Hurt by hard riding, she was put out in the meadow to see if the rest would help her. Lord George had been careless with

Ginger. We couldn't gallop about any longer, but we would feed and lie down together. We stood for hours with our heads close to each other until our family returned from town.

One day, the master came into the meadow with Mr. York. They looked at Ginger and me, and seemed quite upset.

"These horses belonged to my old friend. I promised him a good home, and look what I've given them! The mare should be okay after a long rest, but I'm afraid I must sell the black one. I can't have a horse in my stable with knees like these."

Mr. York agreed. "I know a man in Bath with stables. He often looks for a good horse at a low price. He is good to them. I will check into it."

The two men left, leaving Ginger and me very sad.

"They'll soon take you away," said Ginger, "and I shall lose the only friend I have. Most likely, we will never see each other again."

A week later, a man came into the meadow, and I was sold to the man Mr. York had spoken about. I found myself in a comfortable stable where I was well fed and well groomed. Our master kept a good many horses and carriages for different jobs. Sometimes the horses and carriages were lent out to gentlemen or ladies who wanted to drive themselves.

One day I went out with a driver who had a lady and two children in the carriage with him. He flicked the reins as we started, and hit me with the whip. My driver was laughing with the lady and children and didn't keep an eye on where he was going. So, it wasn't a surprise to me that I got a stone in one of my front feet. Every step I took made the stone stick deeper into my foot. But the man drove me a good half mile before he noticed anything wrong with my step. By that time, I was limping badly and in great pain.

"Now why would they send us out with a lame horse?" the man cried in disgust. He then hit me with the whip, ordering me to keep moving.

About that time, a farmer came riding up on a brown pony and stopped.

"I think there is something wrong with your horse," the farmer said as he came to me and at once lifted my hurt foot.

"Bless me! There's a big stone! This horse is not lame, he just needs someone to pay attention to his step!"

At first, the farmer tried to get it out with his hand. He finally drew a knife out of his pocket and worked on it till it came out. Holding it up, he said, "Look at this stone! It's a wonder he didn't fall down and break his knee!"

"I never knew horses picked up stones," the man said.

"Well, they do," said the farmer. "And if you don't want to hurt this horse further, you will drive him gently for a while. The foot is already bruised so your horse will limp." Then the farmer got back on his pony and trotted away.

When he was gone, my driver flicked the reins and whipped me like he had before. I went on, glad that the stone was gone but still in a lot of pain. This was the sort of treatment we job horses often got.

One type of driver that often hired me out I called the steam engine. These people were used to traveling by train, and they believed a horse was something like a steam engine, only smaller. They thought that when they paid for a horse to do a job, they could take it as far as they wanted, as fast as they wanted, and with as heavy a load as they pleased. It didn't matter if the roads were sloppy and muddy, or stony and dry. To them a horse should go at locomotive speed.

Sometimes I did have the chance to meet up with a good driver, someone who knew horses. One morning, two gentlemen came out. The tallest one came over to pet me. This gentleman took a great liking to me. After riding several more times, he asked my master to sell me to a friend of his. He wanted a safe, pleasant horse for riding. And so it came to pass that I was sold to Mr. Barry that summer.

CHAPTER 12

A Thief

My new master was very busy in his work and knew little about horses. So he rented a stable close to his home and hired a groomer named Filcher. He ordered the best hay, with plenty of oats, crushed beans, bran, and ryegrass. I heard my master give the order myself, so I knew I was well off.

For a few days, all was well. My groomer understood the horse business. He kept the stable clean, he groomed me well, and he was gentle. He used to work in a fine hotel in Bath. He gave that up to grow fruits and vegetables to sell. His wife raised chickens and rabbits.

But after a while, my food began running out. I had the beans, but bran was mixed with them instead of oats. And even those servings were small. In two or three weeks, my strength and mood were suffering. Still, I ate what I was given, which now was grass. But I couldn't keep up my shiny coat without corn. In about two months, I thought for sure my master would notice how I looked. But would he know the problems I had were from poor feeding?

One afternoon, my master rode me into the country to visit a farmer friend. This gentleman had a good eye for horses and looked me over.

"It seems to me, Barry, that your horse looked better when you first got him. Has he been sick?"

"No," said my master, "but he is not nearly as lively as he was. My groomer tells me that horses are always dull and weak in the autumn."

"Fiddlesticks!" said the farmer. "This is only August. What do you feed him?"

My master told him. The other man shook his head and began to feel me all over.

"I don't know who is eating that corn, Barry, but your horse sure isn't getting it. Have you ridden him hard?"

"No, very gently," he said.

"Put your hand here," said the man, passing his hand over my neck and shoulder. "He's as warm and damp as a horse that eats only grass. I hate to think ill of anyone, but maybe your groomer is not doing his job. There are mean scoundrels who would rob animals of their food."

The farmer took me to have a good meal in his stable. It was the best I had eaten in quite a while. I wished I could tell my master where his oats were going. Every morning at about six o'clock, my groomer would come with a little boy who always carried a basket with him. He would go into the back room where the corn was kept. After he filled the bag, he would be off.

Five or six mornings later, just as the boy had left the stable, the door was pushed open and a policeman walked in, holding the child tightly by the arm. Another policeman followed, locking the door on the inside, saying, "Show me the place where your father keeps his rabbits' food."

The boy began to cry and led the policeman to the corn bin. Here the policemen found an empty bag like the one that was full of oats in the boy's basket.

I heard later on that Filcher went to jail for what he did. It was hard for me to feel bad for him, though. He wasn't an honest man.

A new groomer came within a few days. His name was Alfred Smirk and he stroked and petted me when my master was there to see it. He brushed my mane and tail and shined my hooves with oil. But when it came to cleaning my feet, he treated me no better than a cow.

Alfred Smirk spent a good deal of time combing his hair and whiskers and fussing with his necktie. Everyone thought he was such a kind man. I say he was the laziest fellow I ever had the chance to meet. He never cleaned all the straw out of my stall, and the strong smell made my eyes burn. I never felt like eating my food.

One day my master came and said, "Alfred, the stable smells rather bad. Can you give that stall a good scrub and use plenty of water?"

"If you wish," he said. "The horse may catch cold, but I'll do what you ask, sir."

"Well," said my master, "I don't like the smell of the stable. There must be something wrong."

Alfred replied, "The drain sometimes smells bad. There might be something wrong with it."

"I will call on the bricklayer and have him check it," my master said.

But when the bricklayer came, he found nothing wrong with the drain. The smell in my box was as bad as ever. And from standing on wet straw, my feet got sore. My master used to say, "I don't know what is the matter with this horse. He doesn't walk well."

"Yes sir," said Alfred. "I have noticed the same thing when I exercise him."

But the truth is, I was hardly ever exercised. When the master was busy, I often stood for days together without stretching my legs at all. I started to grow fat. I also got restless and feverish many days. Alfred never gave me a dinner of green meal or bran mash, which would have cooled me. Instead, I was given pills and mixtures that were poured down my throat. All they did was make me feel ill and uncomfortable.

One day my feet were so tender that while trotting over fresh stones with my master, I stumbled twice. He was worried and took me to the vet, who looked at my feet, one at a time.

"Your horse has got the 'thrush.' I am sorry to say it's quite bad. His feet are very tender. You are lucky he hasn't fallen down when you were riding. This is the kind of thing we find in dirty stables, where the stall hasn't been swept and fresh hay hasn't been put down. If you send your horse back tomorrow, I will work on his feet and I will teach your groomer how to apply liniment."

The next day, my feet were washed well and soaked in strong lotion. It was not pleasant. The doctor told Alfred to clean out my stall each day and keep the floor very clean. With this treatment, I soon got my lively spirits back. But Mr. Barry was so disgusted with poor groomers that he decided to give me up. So once again, I was sold.

PART III

CHAPTER 13

At the Horse Fair

∽

A horse fair is an exciting event with plenty to see and do. And one can't imagine all the breeds of horses on view. Long lines of young horses from the country and shaggy little Welsh ponies, no taller than Merrylegs were everywhere. And there were a good many like myself, handsome and well bred. Hundreds of cart horses, some with their long tails braided and tied, were displayed. Some horses were showing off their trots to the crowd. This is what one sees out in the open.

Around back, though, things were different.

Some horses were hurting from too much work, with sores on their backs and hips. Their knees and hind legs jerked as they walk. Some were so thin you could see their ribs. Many looked as if there was no more pleasure left in life.

When I came to the fair, I was put with two or three other strong, good-looking horses. A lot of people looked me over, but turned their heads away when they saw my broken knees.

There was a lot of bargaining when the horse sales began. If a horse could speak, though, I would say there were more lies told and more trickery at that horse fair than truths. The man who sold me said it was only from a slip in the stall.

People pulled my mouth open, looked at my eyes, and felt all the way down my legs. They liked to watch me trot. It was funny how different the people were who came to see me: some looked me over in a rough manner, like I was made of wood, while others would move their hands gently over me.

Of course, I was also judging the buyers by how they treated me. There was one man whom I wished would buy me. I knew by how he acted that he was kind to horses. He spoke gently and had a cheery look in his eyes. When he offered a sum of money for me, the dealer turned it down. Then he walked away, and a loud, dreadful man offered the dealer the same amount of money. They were arguing over the price when the man with the kind eyes came back. I reached my head toward him and he stroked my face kindly.

"Well, old boy," he said, "I think we should get along just fine. You seem worth the little bit more he wants."

The salesman and the kind man made a deal, and my new master led me out of the fair. He gave me a good feed of oats and talked to me.

Soon we were on our way to London. By night, we had reached the great city. The gas lamps were already lit. There were streets crossing one another for miles and miles. At last, we came to a long, wooden booth called a cabstand.

"Good night, Governor!" I heard my new master call out.

"Hey!" cried a voice. "Did you get a good one?"

"I think so!" replied my owner.

"I wish you luck with him!"

"Thank you, Governor!" he replied, and rode on.

We soon turned onto a very narrow street with houses on one side and stables on the other. My owner pulled up to one of the houses and whistled. The door flew open. A young woman, followed by a little girl and a boy, ran out as my master dismounted me.

"Open the gates, Harry, and Mother will bring us a lantern."

The next minute, they were all standing around me in the stable.

"Is he gentle, Father?"

"Yes, Dolly, as gentle as your kitten. Come over and pat him."

At once the little hand was patting me on my shoulder without fear. How good it felt!

"Let me give him some bran mash while you rub him down," said the mother.

"That's just what he wants," the man said. "And how about me?" he asked. "Do I get some mash, too?"

The woman smiled. "Sausage dumpling and apple turnover," she said.

My new master's name was Jeremiah Barker, but everyone called him Jerry. Polly, his wife, was a plump little woman with dark hair, dark eyes, and a merry little mouth. Their son Harry was twelve years old, and his sister Dolly was eight. They were a loving family.

I was led into a clean-smelling stall with plenty of dry straw. After a wonderful supper, I lay down, thinking I was going to be happy.

CHAPTER 14

An Old War Horse

಄

Jerry had a cab, or taxi, of his own. His other horse was a tall white animal named Captain. Captain had a proud way of holding his head and was a good-mannered old horse. He told me that when he was young, he was in the war. He belonged to an officer in the cavalry, something we talked about later.

The next morning, Polly brought me a slice of apple, and Dolly gave me a piece of bread. I felt like the "Black Beauty" of old times and tried to show them I was friendly. Polly thought I was a very handsome horse, too nice to be driving around a cab.

"Let's call him Jack, after our old horse," said Jerry.

Captain went out in the cab all morning. Harry came in after school to feed me and give me water. In the afternoon, I was harnessed into the cab. Jerry worked hard to make sure my collar and bridle fit well. What a relief it was to be comfortable as I rode!

After driving through the side street, we came to the cabstand. On one side of this wide street were high houses with shops. On the other side was an old church and yard, surrounded by an iron fence. Alongside the fence, cabs were lined up, waiting for passengers. Bits of hay were strewn on the ground. We pulled in the line behind the last cab. Two or three men came around and began to look at me. They talked for a minute, during which Jerry said some very nice things about me.

Then, up came a jolly-looking man, dressed in a gray coat and pants. His hair was gray, too. He looked me over and said, "He's a good horse, Jerry. I don't know what you paid for him, but he's worth it!"

This man's name was Grant, but he was called "Gray Grant" or "Governor Grant." He was a pleasant man. He seemed to be the one in the group who settled arguments and disagreements.

The first week of my life as a cab horse was difficult. The noise, the hurrying, and the crowds of horses, carts, and carriages made me very nervous. I soon found out, though, that I could trust my driver. After that, I got used to it.

Jerry soon found out that I would do my best. He never whipped me, for he knew I would go on when he wanted. In a short time, my master and I understood each other well.

In the stable, he kept us clean, and gave us

many different feeds and plenty of them. He also gave us lots of fresh water, leaving it by us night and day. But the best thing we enjoyed here was our Sundays for rest. It was then that I learned to love the company of Captain.

Captain had been an army horse, and his first owner was an officer in the Crimean War. His master treated him with great care and kindness. He told me a horse's life in the army was pleasant, but when it came to being sent across the ocean in a ship, he had almost changed his mind.

"Our bodies were strapped and we were lifted off our legs and swung over the water to the deck. We were placed in small stalls and didn't see the sun or sky for a long time. We couldn't even go for walks. The ship rolled about and we were knocked around. We neighed for joy when we once more felt the ground beneath our feet.

"We soon found that the country we had

come to was very different than our own."

"What about the fighting?" I asked. "Weren't you scared?"

"We stood around a lot, waiting to go into battle. As long as we felt our riders firm in our saddles, and their hands steady on the reins, we didn't give way to fear.

"Many horses died, but I still carried on bravely. My master's cheery voice made me feel as if he and we couldn't be killed. When he was guiding me, I never felt terror, until that one day I shall not forget. One autumn morning we heard the firing of the enemy's guns. My dear master and I were at the head of the line. He leaned down and stroked my neck that morning, more than I think he ever had before. He said, 'We shall have a time of it today, Bayard. But we will do our duty as always.'

"We were used to the gunfire in the battles—the cannons, muskets, and heavy guns. But today, it was the worst ever. Many brave men and horses went down. Fearful as it was, no one stopped or turned back. Our group kept getting smaller, but we continued to charge ahead.

"My master was cheering on his soldiers with his right arm raised high, when one of the cannonballs whizzed past my head and hit my master. I felt his sword fall, and then he fell backward. The other riders swept past us, taking me with them.

"I wanted to stay by his side, protecting him from the rush of horses' feet, but I couldn't. Our side had been beaten badly. Some of the horses were walking on three legs, while some fell to the ground, struggling to get back on their feet. The cries of the horses and men were awful to hear.

"After the battle, the wounded men were brought in, and the dead were buried."

"What about the wounded horses?" I asked. "Were they left to die?"

"No, they were helped by the army doctors. But many horses didn't make it back.

"I never saw my dear master again. I believe he died when he fell. I never loved any other master so well. When the war was over, I came back to England."

"People talk about war like it is a noble thing," I said, looking at the brave horse beside me.

"Those people have never really seen war. It is fine when the enemy is far away. But when thousands of brave men and horses are killed or hurt for life, war looks very different."

"Do you know what they fought about?" said I.

"No, a horse can't understand such things. But the enemy must have been very wicked if we went all the way over that ocean to stop them."

CHAPTER 15

Jerry Barker and a London Cab Horse

I never knew a better man than my new master. He was good, kind, and strong. He was so good-tempered and merry that few people could even argue with him. He liked to make up little songs and sing them to himself. One he really liked was this:

"Come, father and mother,
And sister and brother,
Come all of you, turn to
And help one another."

The family did just that. Polly and Dolly would come in the morning to help with the cab, to brush off and beat the cushions and polish the glass. Jerry would give Captain and me a good cleaning in the yard while Harry rubbed the harnesses. There was a great deal of laughing between them, and it put Captain and me in great spirits. We often heard Jerry sing to himself:

"If you in the morning
Throw minutes away,
You can't pick them up
In the course of the day."

One morning a gentleman walked into the yard. "Good morning, Mr. Barker," the man said kindly. "I would like to hire you to take my wife, Mrs. Briggs, to church every Sunday. We go to a church now that is a little too far for her to walk."

"Thank you," said Jerry, "but I only have a license to drive from Monday to Saturday."

"Oh," the man answered, "it would be easy to fix your license. Mrs. Briggs wants only you to drive her."

"I would be happy to help you, sir, but I had a seven-day license before, and the work was too hard for me and my horse. I did not get to see my family much, and I never got to go to church."

"I agree," said the man, "but this short trip would be easy work for you and I am a good customer, remember?"

"Yes, sir, that is true," Jerry said, "and I am grateful for all you do. But please understand why I must turn down the Sunday work. I read that God made man, and He made horses and all the other beasts, and as soon as He made them, He made a day of rest. I know my horse is better after a day of rest, and I think I am also."

"Oh, very well," said the gentleman. "Don't trouble yourself, Mr. Barker. I will find someone else." And he walked away.

Although I was proud of my master for standing firm for our day of rest, Mrs. Briggs stopped calling on us for work. The men Jerry worked with soon found out about him losing his best customer. Most of them said he had made a bad decision, but Jerry stuck to his promise. He answered them with a rhyme: "Just do your best, and leave the rest; 'twill all come right some day or night."

Three weeks after this, late one evening, Polly came running across the road with the lantern. "Mrs. Briggs sent her servant this afternoon to ask you to take her out tomorrow at eleven o'clock. I told her that would be fine. You see, Jerry, Mr. Briggs asked other cabdrivers to take his wife to church, but the mistress says not one cab is as clean as yours and nothing will suit her but your cab."

Jerry broke into a merry laugh. "We knew this would work out!" Jerry said, taking my harness off. After this, Mrs. Briggs wanted Jerry's cab as often as before, but on Sundays he was to rest.

One Sunday morning, Jerry was cleaning me in the yard when Polly came running over. "Poor Dinah Brown just got a letter saying her mother is very sick. Dinah must go to her right away. She says that if she takes the train, that would be impossible! Her new baby is only four weeks old. If you take her in your cab, she promises to pay you well."

"It's not the money I am thinking about," Jerry said. "I was wondering about losing our Sunday together. The horses are tired and so am I."

"Your family will be fine," Polly said. "Wouldn't you want someone to do this for us if my mother was very sick and I needed to see her?"

"Polly, tell Dinah we will leave by ten. While I get ready, ask Butcher Braydon if he would lend me his light, high-wheeled carriage. It will make it easier for the horse."

Soon she returned, saying that Jerry could borrow the lighter carriage. Polly then brought Jerry some bread and cheese, promising a good meal when he got back.

I was chosen for the journey. It was a fine May day, and the light, big-wheeled cart ran easily. As soon as we were out of the town, the smell of the fresh grass and the country roads were as pleasant as in old times.

Dinah's family lived in a small farmhouse, close by a meadow with shady trees. There were two cows feeding there. "If your cows don't mind, I know my horse would just love some time in your meadow. He's quiet and it would be a special treat for him."

"Please help yourself to anything," the young man answered. "After your kindness to my sister, we want you to have the best. We will be having some dinner in an hour. I hope you'll come in."

Jerry thanked him kindly, but told him he'd brought some lunch with him. When my harness was taken off, I didn't know what I should do first—whether to eat the grass, or roll over on my back, or lie down and rest, or gallop across the meadow to celebrate being free. I decided to do everything.

Jerry seemed to be as happy as I was. He sat down by a bank under a shady tree and listened to the birds. Then he sang to himself, read out of a little brown book he always carried, and wandered around the meadow and down by a little brook. Afterward, he picked some wildflowers and tied them together with long strands of ivy. Then he gave me a good lunch of oats that he had brought with him. But the time seemed all too short—I had not been in a field since I left poor Ginger.

We came home gently. Jerry's first words

when we got home were, "Well, Polly, I haven't lost my Sunday after all, for the birds were singing hymns in every bush, and I joined in the service. And Jack, well, he was like some young colt."

Jerry thought for a moment. "Perhaps I won't get rich," he mused, "but I will still be happy knowing that my horse and I have helped people."

When he handed Dolly the flowers, she jumped about for joy.

CHAPTER 16

Poor Ginger

∾

One day, a shabby old cab drove up beside ours as we stood waiting for customers. The horse was an old, worn-out chestnut with a dirty coat and bones showing through its coat. The knees were a mess, and its front legs were wobbly. I had been eating some hay and the wind rolled a little clump that way. The poor animal put out her long, thin neck and picked it up. Then she looked about for more. As I was trying to think about where I had seen that horse before, she looked right at me and said, "Black Beauty, is that you?"

It was Ginger—but how she had changed! The beautifully arched neck was now straight. Her legs were swollen from hard work. The face that was once so full of spirit and happiness was now full of suffering. I could tell by the heaving of her sides and her cough how bad her breathing had become.

I stepped closer to my old friend and asked her how she was. She had a sad story to tell. After I left, she had stayed at the home where we were together for another year. Then she was fit for work again and was sold once more. For a little while, she did very well. But after riding hard again, she soon became sore all over. After she had rested there awhile, she was sold another time, and many times after that.

"And so, at last," she sighed, "I was bought by a man who keeps a lot of cabs and horses, and rents them out. I cannot tell you how awful my life has been. They whip me and work me hard, never thinking about how I suffer. I work all week, with never a Sunday off."

"What happened, Ginger? You used to stand up for yourself if you weren't treated right."

"Ah," she said, "I did once, but it's no use. Men are stronger, and if they are mean and without feeling, there is nothing we can do. I hate to suffer another day. But you look well, and I am glad for you."

I put my nose up to hers, but I could say nothing to make her feel better. I do think she was pleased to see me, for she said, "You are the only friend I ever had."

Just then, her driver came up, and with a tug at her mouth, he drove her off, leaving me very sad indeed.

A short time after that, a cart with a dead horse in it passed by our cabstand. It was an old chestnut with a long, thin neck. I saw the white streak down her forehead. I believe it was Ginger. I hoped it was, for then her troubles would be over.

CHAPTER 17

Old Captain and His Successor

The cabs were busy, and we hadn't yet eaten our lunch, when a poor young woman carrying a heavy child came along the street. She asked Jerry if he knew the way to the St. Thomas Hospital. She was a stranger in London and her child was sick.

"Poor fellow," she said, "he is in a great deal of pain. If I could get him into the hospital, he might get well. Sir, how far is it?"

"I'm sorry, missus," Jerry said, "but you can't get there walking through these crowds. It is three miles away and that child is heavy!"

"Yes, but I am strong and if I knew the way, I could get there."

"No, you can't," said Jerry. "You could be knocked down. Look, get into this cab and I'll drive you to the hospital. And hurry, the rain is on its way."

"No, sir," she said. "I can't do that. I only have enough money to get back home. Please tell me the way."

"Look here, missus," Jerry said. "I've got a wife and dear children at home. Now you get into that cab. I'll take you there for free. I'd be ashamed of myself to take any money from you."

"Heaven bless you!" the woman said, bursting into tears. Jerry helped the woman and her son into his cab.

As Jerry went to open the door, two officials of the town ran up calling out, "Cab!"

"Engaged," cried Jerry. Ignoring him, both

men pushed past the woman and sprang into the cab. Jerry looked as stern as a policeman. "This cab is *engaged*, sirs, by that lady." When they understood Jerry's intent, they got out, calling him all sorts of bad names.

"Thank you a thousand times," the woman said when they arrived at the hospital. "I could never have gotten here alone!"

"You're kindly welcome, and I hope the dear child will get better soon."

As he watched the woman and her child enter the hospital, Jerry said how pleased he was to have helped someone in their time of need. He patted my neck. I think I know how he felt.

The rain was coming down fast, now. Just as we were leaving the hospital, I heard someone call for a cab. We stopped, and a lady came down the steps. Jerry seemed to know her at once. She pushed back her hat and said, "Jeremiah Barker! Is it you?" As she got closer, she said, "You are just the friend I want. It's so very difficult to get a cab in this part of London today."

"I would be happy to take you, ma'am. Where would you like to go?"

"To Paddington Station, please. And if we have the time, I would love to hear about Polly and the children."

We got to the station in good time, and the lady stood a good while talking to Jerry. I found out she had been Polly's mistress. After asking many questions about her, the woman said, "How is the cab work in the winter? I know your wife worried about you last year."

"Yes. I had a bad cough that stayed with me into spring. But I am getting on pretty well. I wouldn't know what to do if I didn't have a horse to look after."

"Well, Barker," she said, "it is awful to risk your health in this work. If you ever decide to give up cab work, let me know." Then she put something into his hand, saying, "Divide this between the two children. Polly will know how to spend it."

Jerry thanked her and seemed very pleased. We left the station and hurried home to rest.

One day, Captain and Jerry saw two strong horses running quickly in a light carriage, being whipped all the while. Jerry watched in horror as the carriage and horses headed straight for them. Within a moment, the horses were pushed up against the cab. Both wheels were torn off, and the cab was thrown over. Captain was dragged down. Jerry was thrown, too, but miraculously only got bruised. When poor Captain got up, he was cut badly. Jerry led him home gently.

It turned out the driver of the carriage was

very drunk. He had to pay for the damage he caused our master, but there was no one to pay damages to poor Captain.

Jerry and his men did the best they could to make Captain comfortable.

Everyone felt bad for Captain and Jerry. At first, Captain did well, but he was a very old horse. Finally, Jerry decided that the kindest thing to do to Captain would be to put him out of his pain. The next day, one of the men took me to town for some new shoes. When I returned, Captain was gone. The family and I all felt the loss very much.

Jerry soon heard of a valuable young horse who had run away and done some damage. The coachman had orders to look around and sell him for as much as he could get.

"I can do with some high spirits," said Jerry. "As long as he isn't mean."

"There isn't a bit of meanness in him," said the man. "His mouth is very tender, and I think that's what caused him to act wild. He had a bearing rein on, and I believe it made the horse mad."

The next day, Hotspur—that was his name—came home. He was a fine brown horse without a white hair on him. He was as tall as Captain and only five years old.

Jerry patted and talked to him a lot, and soon they understood each other. Jerry said that with an easy bit and plenty of work, he would become as gentle as a lamb.

Hotspur didn't like the idea of going from a carriage horse to a cab horse. He felt he was being looked down upon. But at the end of the first week, he told me that it was worth the move to be treated so well by Jerry. In fact, he settled in well and Jerry liked him very much.

CHAPTER 18

Jerry's New Year

Christmas and the New Year are very happy times for some people. But for cabmen and cabmen's horses, it is no holiday. The work is hard, and you often work late into the night. While merry people are dancing away to the music, I wonder if they ever think of the weary cabman waiting in his carriage, or the mighty horses standing with their legs stiff from the cold.

I was the horse chosen for most of the evening work. We had a great deal of work during the Christmas week. Jerry's cough was bad. But no matter how late we were, Polly sat up for him and came with the lantern to meet him.

On the evening of the New Year, we took two gentlemen to a house in one of the West End squares. We left them off at nine o'clock, and as the clock struck eleven, we were at the door to pick them up.

The wind came on strong, with sleet mixing in with it, and there was no shelter. Jerry got off his high seat and pulled my blanket up tighter around me. Then he walked up and down around me, stamping his feet to get some warmth. By the time the clock struck half past twelve, Jerry rang the bell at the house. He asked the servant if he would still be wanted that night.

"Oh yes, you'll be wanted," said the man. "You must not go—it will soon be over." So Jerry sat down again, but his voice was hoarse and I could barely hear him.

At one fifteen, the two gentlemen came out,

got into the cab without a word, and told Jerry where to drive. My legs were numb with cold and I thought I would stumble as I carried those gentlemen two miles! When they got out, they never said they were sorry to have kept us waiting so long. Instead, they were angry because they didn't like paying for the extra two hours. That night, the money my master earned wasn't worth the suffering we went through.

At last we got home. Jerry could hardly speak, and his cough was dreadful. Polly asked no questions, but opened the door and held the lantern for him.

"Can't I do something?" she asked.

"Yes, get Jack something warm and then boil me soup."

Jerry talked in a scratchy whisper. He could barely get his breath, but he still gave me a rubdown as he always did. He even went up in the hayloft for an extra bundle of straw for my bed.

Polly brought me some warm grain that made me comfortable; then they locked the door.

It was late the next morning before anyone came, and then it was only Harry. He didn't whistle or sing like he always did. At noon, he came again. This time Dolly came with him and she was crying. From what I could tell, Jerry was very sick.

Two days passed. We saw only Harry and sometimes Dolly, since Polly had to stay by Jerry's side. On the third day, while Harry was in the stable, there was a soft tap at the door. Governor Grant came in.

"I won't bother anyone up at the house," he said to Harry, "but I was wondering how Jerry was."

"He is very bad," said Harry. "He can't get much worse. They call it bronchitis. The doctor thinks it will turn one way or another tonight."

"That's very bad," agreed the Governor, shaking his head. "I know two men who died of that last week. But let's hope for the best for your father! If there's any rule that good men should get over these things, I'm sure he will; he's the best man I know. I'll look in on him early tomorrow."

Early next morning he was there. "Well?" he said.

"Father is better," said Harry. "Mother hopes he will get over it."

"Thank goodness!" said the Governor. "Now you must keep him warm, and keep him from worrying about the horses . . . You see, Jack will be fine with a week of rest in a warm stable. You can take him up and down the road to stretch his legs. But this young one . . . if he does not get work, he will get wild. He will be too much for you, and when he does go out, there may be an accident."

"It's like that now," said Harry. "He's so full of spirit that I don't know what to do with him."

"I thought so," said the Governor. "Now, please tell your mother that if she agrees, I will come for him every day. I will work him, and whatever he earns, I will give your mother half of it. That will help out with the horse's feed. I'll come at noon and hear what she has to say." Without waiting for Harry's thanks, he was gone.

At noon, he and Harry came to the stable together. They harnessed Hotspur and took him out.

For a week or more he came for Hotspur. When Harry thanked him, or said anything about his kindness, he laughed it off and said his own horses needed a little rest anyway.

Jerry slowly got better, but the doctor said he could never go back to cab work again. The family talked many times about what they would do for money.

One afternoon, Hotspur was brought in very wet and dirty.

"The streets are nothing but slush," said the Governor.

While Harry was sponging the mud from Hotspur's body and legs, Dolly came in, bubbling with joy.

"Who lives at Fairstowe, Harry? Mother got a letter from Fairstowe. She seemed very happy about it and ran upstairs to tell Father."

"That is Mrs. Fowler's place. Remember when Father met her last summer and she sent you and me money? She was Mother's old mistress."

"Oh, I remember now. But I wonder what she is writing Mother about."

"Mother wrote to her last week," said Harry. "You know, she had told Father if he ever gave up the cab work, she would like to be told. Go and see what she says, Dolly."

Harry continued to rub away at Hotspur. In a few minutes, Dolly came dancing into the stable.

"Oh, Harry, Mrs. Fowler says we are all to go

and live near her! There is an empty cottage that will be perfect for us. It has a garden, and a hen-house, and apple trees, and everything! Her coachman is going to go away in the spring, and she will want Father to take his place. There are good families around, where you could work in a garden or stable or even at the main house. And there's a good school for me. Mother is laughing and crying at the same time. And Father . . . he looks so happy!"

"That's wonderful!" Harry said.

It was quickly settled that as soon as Jerry was well enough, they would move to the country. The cab and the horses were to be sold as soon as possible. This was big news for me, for I was not young anymore. My three years of cab work, even under the best conditions, had been hard. I felt I needed a rest and that I was not the horse I had been.

Mr. Grant said that he would take Hotspur.

And he promised to find a home for me where I should be comfortable.

The day came soon when we would leave. Jerry had not been allowed to go out yet, and I never saw him after that New Year's Eve. Polly and the children came to tell me good-bye. They all wished they could take me with them. Polly put her hand on my mane and her face close to my neck. "Poor old Jack," she said. Dolly was crying. Harry stroked me softly, but said nothing. They all seemed very sad as I was led away to my new place.

PART IV

CHAPTER 19

Jakes and the Lady

I was sold to a corn dealer and baker. Jerry knew the man and thought I would be fed well and not overworked. He was right about the food. And he would have been right about the workload, too, if my master were always watching over me. But many times, when I already had a full load, the foreman would order something else be taken along. My stable man, Jakes, often said I carried too much. But the foreman said there was no use making two trips when we could do it in one.

Jakes always had the bearing rein up. After

three or four months, I could tell it was doing its worst to me.

One day, I was loaded up more than usual, and part of the road was a steep hill. I used all my strength, but I still couldn't make it. I had to keep stopping. This did not please my driver, and he hit me with his whip, badly. "Get going, you lazy fellow," he said, "or I will make you!"

Again I started the heavy load up the hill. I struggled for a few yards, and the whip hit me again. What hurt the worst, though, was doing my very best and still being punished for it. Finally, the driver began hitting me harder and harder, and he wouldn't stop. A lady passerby stepped up to him and pleaded in a sweet voice, "Oh, do not whip your good horse anymore! I am sure he is doing all he can, and the road is very steep. I am sure he is doing his best!"

"If he is doing his best, then he needs to try harder," said Jakes.

"But isn't that a heavy load for a horse?" she asked.

"Yes, too heavy," he said, "but that's not my fault. The foreman came just as we were starting, putting on three hundred more pounds. I must get on with it."

He was raising the whip again when the woman cried out, "Stop! I think I can help you if you let me."

The man laughed.

"You see," she said, "he can't use all his power with his head held back in that bearing rein. If you would take it off, I am sure he would do better. Please try," she said. "I would be very happy if you would."

"Well," said Jakes, "anything to please a lady. How far do you want it down, ma'am?"

"All the way down."

The rein was taken off, and in a moment, I put my head to my knees. How comfortable it was!

Then I tossed it up and down several times to get the stiffness out of my neck.

"Poor fellow! That is what you wanted," she said, patting me with her gentle hand. "And now, I believe he will do better for you."

Jakes took the rein. "Come on, Blackie."

I put my head down and threw all my weight against the collar. I used all my strength and carried that load up the hill.

The lady had walked alongside us. "You see, he did exactly what you wanted once you gave him the chance. You won't put that rein on him again, will you?"

"Well, ma'am," Jakes started, "he did do better once I took it off. And I can promise you, the next time he has a heavy load, I will take it off again. But I couldn't let him go without one all the time. It's the style, you know."

"Wouldn't you rather start a great fashion than try to follow a bad one? A lot of gentlemen don't use bearing reins now. Our carriage horses have not worn them for fifteen years. They don't get as tired as the ones that have them.

"Besides," she added gravely, "we have no right to harm any of God's creatures, do we? They can't talk to us, but it doesn't mean they don't feel pain. Well, thank you for trying my plan. I'm sure you will find this trick far better than using the whip. Good day, now!"

And with that, the lady gave me another soft pat on my neck, and then stepped lightly out of my path. I didn't see her again.

"Now that was a real lady," Jakes said to himself. "She spoke as polite as if I were a rich gentleman. And I will try it her way, at least when we are going uphill."

I must say that, from that day on, he always loosened the reins for hills, but my loads were still heavy. I got so weary from my work that a younger horse was bought in my place. Instead of being put to work, I was left in my cramped stable with only one small window at the end. This left me lonesome and also weakened my eyesight. When I was suddenly brought out into the daylight, it was very painful to my eyes. Several times I stumbled, and could hardly see where I was going.

I believe if I would have stayed there much longer, I would have gone totally blind. Thank goodness I escaped without injury, and was soon sold to a large cab owner.

CHAPTER 20

Farmer Thoroughgood
and His Grandson

∽

I shall never forget my new master. He had black eyes and a pointed nose. His mouth was as full of teeth as a bulldog's. And his voice was as harsh as the grinding of carriage wheels on stones. His name was Nicholas Skinner.

I had heard men say before that seeing is believing. But I should say that feeling is believing, for I never knew what misery was until then.

Skinner took no care of his cabs or men. Most of the men who worked there were hard on the cabs and the horses. In this place, we had no Sunday rest, even in the heat of the summer.

Sometimes on a Sunday morning, a group of men would hire the cab for the day—four of them inside and another man with the driver. I had to take them ten or fifteen miles out into the country and back again. None of them ever got out to walk up a hill, no matter how steep or how hot it was. Occasionally, I wouldn't go up. I was too feverish or worn out to move. Only then would the driver call them out to walk.

When I got back to the stable, I was so tired sometimes that I wouldn't touch my food. How I used to long for the nice bran mash that Jerry would give us on Saturday nights in hot weather! It would cool us down and make us so comfortable. Then we would have two nights and one whole day for rest. On Monday morning, we would be as fresh as young horses again.

But here, with no rest, my driver was just as

mean as his master. He had a cruel whip with something so sharp at the end that it often caused me to bleed. He would even whip me under my belly and flip the whip so it hit my head. This took much out of me. But still, I did my best and never hung back. As Ginger used to tell me, it was no use putting up a fight: men are the strongest.

My life was so awful now that on some days I wished I would die at work, just to be out of my misery. One day, my wish almost came true.

I went on the cabstand at eight in the morning. I had done a good bit of work when we had to take someone to the railway station. A long train would be coming in, so my driver pulled up in the back of the line like so many other cabs did. It was a full train, and as most of the other cabs were called for, we soon had our turn. It was a group of four: a loud, noisy man with a lady and two children—one boy and one girl. They had a lot of luggage as well. The lady and the boy got into the cab.

While the man yelled orders to my driver about the luggage, the young girl came and looked at me.

"Papa," she said, "this poor horse can't take all our luggage. He is so weak and worn out. Look at him!"

"Oh, he's all right, miss," said my driver. "He's strong enough."

The porter from the train said there was so much luggage to take that the man should hire two cabs.

"Can your horse do it or not?" said the grumpy father.

"Oh, he can do it all right," said the driver.

"Papa, please," the little girl cried. "Take another cab. This is so unfair to the horse!"

"Nonsense, Grace. Get in at once and don't make all this fuss. The driver knows his horse!"

My little friend had to obey, while box after

box was loaded on top of the cab. At last, all was ready, and we drove off.

The load was very heavy, and I did pretty well until we came to Ludgate Hill. It was there that my heavy load and my weary body stopped me. The driver hit me hard with the whip. Then, I lost my footing and fell to the ground on my side. The fall took all the breath out of my body.

I lay perfectly still and heard loud noises around me. I heard one man say, "He's dead. He will never get up again." Still, I didn't open my eyes. I could only take a gasping breath now and then. Cold water was thrown on my head and some medicine was poured into my mouth. A blanket covered my still body.

A man with a kind voice stroked my neck and told me to try to get up. I tried very hard to stand. Finally on the third try, I got to my feet and was led gently into a nearby stable. Here, good food was brought to me, and I ate the warm gruel thankfully.

In the evening, I felt good enough to go back to Skinner's stables. A doctor examined me and said, "If you would let him rest for six months, he would be ready to work again. But right now, there is no strength left in him."

"Then I'll get rid of him!" barked Skinner. "He might get better, he might not. I work them as long as they can go, then I sell them for what I can fetch."

"There is a sale of horses coming in about ten days. If you rest him and feed him well, he may get better and fetch you a good price."

Skinner gave orders for me to be well fed and cared for. It made me so much better! I began to look forward to being sold. Any change from here had to be an improvement. So I held up my head and hoped for the best.

Of course, at this sale I found myself with all the other broken-down horses. There were some there that I couldn't imagine anyone buying.

The men and women there, buyers and sellers, looked as poor as most of the horses. There were old men with only a few dollars trying to buy horses to drag around carts. Some other old men were trying to sell horses that weren't, in my opinion, worth anything. There were other buyers, though, whom I would have willingly used my last strength in serving. They had kind voices who I could trust. There was one tottering old man who took a great fancy to me, but I was not strong enough for his work. I was very worried about what would become of me.

In a while, I noticed a gentleman farmer with a young boy at his side. He had wide shoulders and a kind face, and wore a wide-brimmed hat. When he came over to me, he stood still and gave me a sad look. I pricked up my ears and looked at him.

"There's a horse, Willie, who has seen better days."

"Poor old fellow!" said the boy. "Grandpapa, do you think he was ever a carriage horse?"

"Oh, yes, my boy!" said the farmer, coming closer. "Look at his nostrils and his ears, the shape of his neck and shoulders. That horse came from a good family line." He put out his hand and gave me a kind pat on the neck. I put out my nose in answer to his kindness. The boy stroked my face.

"See, Grandpapa, how well he understands kindness? Could you buy him and make him young again, just like you did with Ladybird?"

"My dear boy, I can't make all old horses young. Besides, Ladybird was not so old. She was just run down and badly overworked."

"Well, Grandpapa, look at his mane and tail. He is very thin, but his eyes are not sunken like some old horses. Please, Grandpapa, ask the price.

I am sure he would grow young in your meadow."

The man who had brought me for sale now put in his word. "The young gentleman is smart, sir. The fact is, this horse was overworked pulling cabs. I heard the vet say that a six-month rest would make him right again. I have taken care of him these past two weeks, and I have never met a more pleasant horse. Pay this small price for him now, and he'll be worth double that next spring."

The old gentleman laughed and the little boy looked up eagerly.

The farmer slowly felt my legs, which were strained and swollen. Then he looked at my mouth. "Thirteen or fourteen years old, I say. Can you walk him around a bit?"

I arched my poor, thin neck, raised my tail a little, and threw out my stiff legs as well as I could.

"What is the lowest you will take for him?" said the farmer as I came back.

"The price I told you is firm, sir."

"I hope I'm not making a mistake," the man said, digging in his pocket. "Can you take him to the inn for me?"

"Yes sir," the seller said. They walked forward, and I was led behind. The boy could hardly contain his happiness. The old gentleman seemed just as pleased. I had a good feed at the inn and was then gently ridden home by a man who worked for my new master. When I got there, I was turned loose in a large meadow with a shed in one corner of it.

My new master, Mr. Thoroughgood, gave orders that I should have hay and oats every night and morning. He also said I should have free run of the meadow all day. His son Willie was in charge of my care.

The boy was proud of his job, and there wasn't a day that he didn't come to see me. He always came with kind words and softly patted my neck. Of course, I grew to love him very much. He called me Old Crony, because I used to come to the gate and follow him about. Sometimes he brought his grandfather, who always looked closely at my legs.

The rest, the good food, the soft grass, and the gentle exercise soon began to help my health and my spirits. During the winter my legs improved so much that I really did start to feel young again. One day in March, Mr. Thoroughgood noticed that my legs were no longer stiff.

"He's growing young, Willie. We must give him a little gentle work now, and by midsummer, he will be as good as Ladybird. He has a beautiful mouth and steps well. We couldn't have hoped for better."

"Oh, Grandpapa, I am so glad you bought him!"

"So am I, my boy, but he has you to thank more than me. We must start looking for a quiet place for him where he will be valued."

CHAPTER 21

My Last Home

༺

One day during the summer, the groomer cleaned and dressed me with such special care that I thought I was going to be sold. He trimmed my coat, ran a brush over my hooves, and even parted and combed my mane. He went so far as polishing my harness before putting it on me.

Willie seemed excited as he squeezed into the carriage with his grandfather.

"If the ladies like him," said the old gentleman, "it will be perfect."

We were about a mile from the village when

we came to a pretty house with a lawn and shrubbery at the front and a driveway going right up to the door. Willie rang the doorbell and asked if Miss Blomefield or Miss Ellen was at home. They were indeed.

Mr. Thoroughgood went inside while Willie waited outside with me. In about ten minutes he returned, followed by three ladies. A tall, pale lady, wrapped in a white shawl, leaned on a younger lady with dark eyes and a merry face. The third lady was a very elegant woman named Miss Blomefield. They all came and looked at me and asked questions. The younger lady, Miss Ellen, really seemed to like me. She said I had a wonderful face. But the tall, pale lady said she would be nervous riding a carriage pulled by this horse. If he fell once, he may do it again, she objected.

"But you see, ladies," Mr. Thoroughgood explained, "many excellent horses have had their knees broken because they had careless drivers. It is

not their fault at all. That's what I see in this horse.
If you would like to try him out for a while it would
be fine. Your coachman can give you his opinion."

"You have always been wise when it comes to
horses," said the elegant lady, "so your suggestion
to try this horse matters a lot to me. If my sister
Lavinia doesn't mind, we will accept your offer
and try him out."

The group decided I would be sent for the
very next day.

In the morning, a smart-looking young man
came for me. At first he looked pleased, but when
he saw my knees, he said in a disappointed voice,
"I am surprised that you would try to sell a horse
with such bad knees."

"You are only trying him out," Mr. Thoroughgood reminded him. "If he is not as safe as any
horse you have ever driven, then send him back."

I was led to my new home, placed in a comfortable stable, fed, and left to myself. The next

day, when my groomer was cleaning my face he exclaimed, "That is just like the star Black Beauty had! He is about the same height, too. I wonder where he is now."

A little farther on, he came to the place on my neck where I had been bled and a little knot was left in the skin. He stepped back and looked curiously at me. He began feeling me all over and said to himself, "White star in the forehead, one white foot, and this little knot in just that place . . ." He then looked at the middle of my back. "As sure as I'm alive, there's that little patch of white hair John used to call 'Beauty's three-penny bit.' It must be Beauty! Do you know me? Little Joe Green, who almost killed you?" And he began patting and patting me as if he was quite overjoyed.

I could not say that I remembered him, for now he was a fine, grown-up young man with black whiskers and a man's voice. But I was glad he remembered me and that he was Joe Green. I put my nose up to him and tried to say that we were friends. I never saw a man so pleased.

"Give you a fair try? I should say so! I wonder, who was the nasty one who broke your knees, my old Beauty? You must have been treated horribly somewhere. Well, you certainly will be treated fine here, old boy! I only wish John Manly was here to see you."

In the afternoon, I was harnessed onto a low carriage and brought to the ladies' door. Miss Ellen was going to try me, and Mr. Green went with her. Soon she seemed pleased with my trot. I heard Joe telling her about me, and how he was sure I was Squire Gordon's old Black Beauty.

When we returned, the other sisters came out to hear how I had behaved myself. Miss Ellen told them what she had just heard. She said, "I shall certainly write to Mrs. Gordon and tell her that her favorite horse has come to us. How pleased she will be!"

After this, I was driven every day for a week or so. Since I appeared to be safe, Miss Lavinia at last went for a ride in a small carriage. They decided to keep me and to call me by my old name of "Black Beauty."

I have now lived in this happy place for a whole year. Joe is the best and the kindest of groomers. My work is easy and pleasant, and I feel my strength and spirits coming back. Mr. Thoroughgood remarked to Joe the other day, "In your place, he will live to be twenty years old, maybe more."

Willie always speaks to me when he can and treats me as his special friend. My ladies have promised me that I shall never be sold again, so I have nothing to fear.

And so my story ends. My troubles are all over, and I am finally home. Sometimes, before I am fully awake, I imagine myself to be back in the orchard at Birtwick, standing with my old friends under the apple trees.

Questions, Questions, Questions
by Arthur Pober, Ed.D.

❧

Have you ever been around a toddler who keeps asking the question "Why?" Does your teacher call on you in class with questions from your homework? Do your parents ask you questions at the dinner table about your day ? We are always surrounded by questions that need a specific response. But is it possible to have a question with no right answer?

The following questions are about the book you just read. But this is not a quiz! They are designed to help you look at the people, places, and events in the story from different angles. These questions do not have specific answers. Instead, they might make you think of the story in a completely new way.

Think carefully about each question and enjoy discovering more about this classic story.

1. *Black Beauty* is told from the unique perspective of a horse. How long did it take you to realize that the narrator was an animal? Have you read other books that were told by animals? How does *Black Beauty* compare to them?

2. How does the fact that Black Beauty is telling the story affect the way the scenes of cruelty are depicted? Would it have been as powerful a story if it was told from the human point of view?

3. Why are the horses willing to follow James out of the burning stable? Have you ever had a pet that would follow you anywhere?

4. Trust plays an important role in *Black Beauty*. How is Black Beauty's trust betrayed? How is it rewarded?

5. Why does John react as he does when Tom Green calls him ignorant? Do you agree with his reaction? What would you have said to Tom?

6. What happens to make Black Beauty realize that Joe will always protect him from harm? How does this event change Joe "at once from a boy to a man"? Have you ever experienced such a life-altering event? What was it?

7. Why is the bearing rein used on the horses? Can you think of any fashionable clothing that humans used to wear even though it made them uncomfortable? What about today?

8. How did Ginger's attitude toward beatings change? Do you think she gave up, or was she still looking out for her own best interest?

9. Jerry takes every Sunday off with one exception. Do you agree with his reasons for only

working six days a week? Why did he give in and work one Sunday? Would you have done the same?

10. In many ways, Black Beauty's life comes full circle. By the end of the book, he is once again in a good home and under the care of Joe Green. How has their time apart changed Beauty from the horse Joe used to know? How has the time changed Joe? In what ways have the two remained the same?

Afterword

❦

First impressions are important.

Whether we are meeting new people, going to new places, or picking up a book unknown to us, first impressions count for a lot. They can lead to warm, lasting memories or can make us shy away from any future encounters.

Can you recall your own first impressions and earliest memories of reading the classics?

Do you remember wading through pages and pages of text to prepare for an exam? Or were you the child who hid under the blanket to read with a flashlight, joining forces with Robin Hood to save Maid Marian? Do you remember only how long it took you to read a lengthy novel such as *Little Women*? Or did you become best friends with the March sisters?

Even for a gifted young reader, getting through long chapters with dense language can easily become overwhelming and can obscure the richness of the story and its characters. Reading an abridged, newly crafted version of a classic novel can be the gentle introduction a child needs to explore the characters and story line without the frustration of difficult vocabulary and complex themes.

Reading an abridged version of a classic novel gives the young reader a sense of independence and the satisfaction of finishing a "grown-up" book. And when a child is engaged with and inspired by a classic story, the tone is set for further exploration of the story's themes, characters, history, and details. As a child's reading skills advance, the desire to tackle the original, unabridged version of the story will naturally emerge.

If made accessible to young readers, these stories can become invaluable tools for understanding themselves in the context of their families and social environments. This is why the Classic Starts series includes questions that stimulate discussion regarding the impact and social relevance of the characters and stories today. These questions can foster lively conversations between children and their parents or teachers. When we look at the issues, values, and standards of past times in terms of how we live now, we can appreciate literature's classic tales in a very personal and engaging way.

Share your love of reading the classics with a young child, and introduce an imaginary world real enough to last a lifetime.

DR. ARTHUR POBER, ED.D.

Dr. Arthur Pober has spent more than twenty years in the fields of early-childhood and gifted education. He is the former principal of one of the world's oldest laboratory schools for gifted youngsters, Hunter College Elementary School, and former director of Magnet Schools for the Gifted and Talented for more than 25,000 youngsters in New York City.

Dr. Pober is a recognized authority in the areas of media and child protection and is currently the U.S. representative to the European Institute for the Media and European Advertising Standards Alliance.